Closer Than Ever

TWO of a kind ™

Closer Than Ever

by Judy Katschke

from the series created by
Robert Griffard
& Howard Adler

📖 HarperEntertainment
An Imprint of **HarperCollins***Publishers*

A PARACHUTE PRESS BOOK

A PARACHUTE PRESS BOOK

Parachute Publishing, L.L.C.
156 Fifth Avenue
Suite 302
New York, NY 10010

Published by
HarperEntertainment
An Imprint of HarperCollins*Publishers*
10 East 53rd Street, New York, NY 10022-5299

TWO OF A KIND books created and produced by Parachute Press, L.L.C., in cooperation with Dualstar Publications, a division of Dualstar Entertainment Group, LLC, published by HarperEntertainment, an imprint of HarperCollins Publishers.

ISBN 0-06-009321-8

First printing: October 2002

Printed in the United States of America

Visit HarperEntertainment on the World Wide Web at
www.harpercollins.com

10 9 8 7 6 5 4 3 2 1

CHAPTER ONE

"Is that a new sweater, Ashley?" Mary-Kate Burke asked her sister during lunch on Friday. "It's so cool!"

"Thanks," Ashley said, glancing at her coral top. "But it isn't new. I got it over a month ago."

Mary-Kate stared at the sweater. *Weird,* she thought. *I don't remember ever seeing it before.* "Oh, well," she said with a shrug. "It's still awesome."

Mary-Kate smiled as she took a bite of her tuna sandwich. Lunch always seemed to taste better when she ate with Ashley. And it was the first time she and Ashley had gotten to eat together in weeks. That's because their first year at the White Oak Academy for Girls was jam-packed. There were

1

classes, tons of homework, clubs, and sports. And sometimes they even had dates with the guys from Harrington, the all-boys school down the road!

"How are your soccer games coming along, Mary-Kate?" Ashley asked, lifting her turkey sandwich to her mouth.

"Soccer?" Mary-Kate asked. "Soccer ended last week."

"Are you serious?" Ashley cried. "Why didn't you tell me? I didn't get a chance to see any of your games and—"

"Okay, time out," Campbell Smith cut in. "What's up with you guys?"

Mary-Kate turned to her roommate. Campbell was sitting next to Phoebe Cahill across the table from her and Ashley. "What do you mean?" she asked.

"I mean, where have you two been?" Campbell asked. She brushed aside the bangs of her short brown hair. "I thought you two knew everything about each other."

"I do," Mary-Kate said. "I know Ashley is twelve and in the First Form like me. She has blond hair, blue eyes—"

"Too easy," Phoebe piped in. Phoebe knew everything about Ashley, too. She was her roommate.

"Okay." Mary-Kate began counting on her fingers. "I know that Ashley likes purple nail polish, ballet, mayonnaise on her turkey sandwiches—"

"I switched to mustard," Ashley interrupted. "And I just ditched my purple polish."

Whoa, Mary-Kate thought. Maybe she didn't know everything there was to know about Ashley. And she was pretty sure she knew why.

"It's been so long since Ashley and I hung out together," Mary-Kate complained. "No wonder we're clueless about each other."

"Mary-Kate is right," Ashley agreed. "I've been so busy, the only person I see on a regular basis is my roommate."

"And what's wrong with that?" Phoebe asked, pretending to look hurt.

"Nothing," Ashley admitted. She turned to Mary-Kate. "It's just that I thought I'd see more of you in boarding school, Mary-Kate, not less. So I'm really starting to miss you."

Mary-Kate felt the same way. Not seeing Ashley was the pits! "I miss you, too, Ashley," she said.

"Okay, okay," Campbell said. "Now that we're all warm and fuzzy, let's get with the program. There's got to be a way for the two of you to spend more time together."

3

"How?" Mary-Kate asked. "I'm on the softball team and in the drama club. . . ."

"I'm on the school paper," Ashley said, "and in the cooking club. . . . "

"And don't forget the Ross Lambert fan club," Phoebe said with a smile.

Ashley blushed. Ross was her boyfriend!

"How can Ashley and I do all those things," Mary-Kate said, "and still hang out together?"

The girls were silent as they thought.

Suddenly Mary-Kate had a major idea. "Hey!" she cried. "What if Ashley and I became roomies? For a whole week!"

"Share a room?" Ashley gasped. "You mean like we did back home in Chicago?"

Mary-Kate nodded. "Remember the time we pitched that tent in the middle of our room?" she asked.

"And tried to roast marshmallows with our hair dryer?" Ashley laughed.

Mary-Kate turned to Campbell and Phoebe. "You guys wouldn't mind rooming together for a week, would you?" she asked.

Campbell and Phoebe looked at each other and shrugged.

"Sounds good to me," Campbell said.

"Me, too," Phoebe said. "But do you think Miss Viola will go for the idea?"

Miss Viola was the housemother at Porter House, the girls' dorm.

"I bet she will," Mary-Kate replied. "Then it will be all systems go!"

"Speaking of going," Ashley said. She took one last bite of her sandwich and stood up. "I've got to run to the Food Management Center and whip up my secret-recipe apple cider for the Harvest Festival tomorrow."

Mary-Kate smiled. Every October White Oak and Harrington celebrated fall in a huge way. For seven days the campus would be jumping with hayrides, pumpkin carving, touch football on the lawn, and the annual apple cider contest.

"You'll win that contest for sure, Ashley," Mary-Kate said. "Your apple cider rules."

"Thanks to my secret recipe," Ashley said.

"Oh, yeah?" Campbell replied. "What's the secret?"

Ashley flashed a mysterious smile. "It's one super-special ingredient," she said. "But if I told you, it wouldn't be a secret recipe."

Mary-Kate watched as Ashley left the dining room. She couldn't wait to start rooming with her sister again!

"You guys, I am so psyched about this," Mary-Kate told her friends. "First thing Ashley and I are going to do is stay up for hours after lights-out—just to catch up."

Phoebe laughed. "You wish."

"What do you mean?" Mary-Kate asked.

"Ashley doesn't stay up late anymore," Phoebe explained. "For the last few months she's been going to bed super-early. Sometimes even before lights-out."

"Really?" Mary-Kate asked. That was new. Was there anything else about Ashley she didn't know?

"Oh, and Ashley's closet is so stuffed with her clothes," Phoebe went on, "it's about to explode!"

"You have lots of clothes, too, Phoebe," Mary-Kate pointed out.

"Vintage clothes don't take up that much room," Phoebe said. "Well, at least it doesn't seem that way."

Phoebe loved dressing in clothes from the 1950s, '60s, and '70s. Even her eyeglass frames were from an antiques boutique.

"Are you sure you want to make the switch, Mary-Kate?" Campbell asked.

"You'll have to be really quiet when Ashley's sleeping. And you'll have nowhere to put your stuff," Phoebe added. "There's still time to get out of it."

"Why would I want to get out of it?" Mary-Kate asked. "Ashley's my sister. And I bet I can get her to change back to the way she was before."

"I bet you can't!" Phoebe said. Her dark curls bobbed as she shook her head.

"Me, too!" Campbell put in.

Mary-Kate wanted to laugh out loud. Were they kidding? Sure she could get Ashley to change. No problem!

"The bet is on," Mary-Kate declared. "First I'll get Ashley to stay up past midnight. Next I'll get her to give away half of her clothes."

"In your dreams!" Campbell cried.

"But you can't tell Ashley about the bet," Phoebe declared. "Not until it's over. It wouldn't be fair. She'd change on purpose to help you."

Mary-Kate gave it a thought. Keeping a secret from Ashley would be hard—especially if they were in the same room. But Mary-Kate was up to the challenge.

"Fine," she said. "But what happens to the loser of the bet . . . or in this case, losers?"

"Let me think," Campbell said. She tapped her chin with one finger. Then she snapped her fingers.

"I know! The loser has to do the winner's laundry for a month. Stinky gym socks and all!"

Mary-Kate gulped when she thought of Campbell's gym socks. Campbell was on a ton of sports teams. Which meant that by the end of the week she had a ton of stinky socks. But what was she thinking? Of course she was going to win!

"Great!" Mary-Kate said with a smile. "But get ready for me to win!"

CHAPTER TWO

"This festival rocks!" Elise Van Hook told Ashley on Saturday morning.

Ashley smiled as she looked around the campus. Students from White Oak and Harrington were crunching through red, yellow, and orange leaves as they munched on candy apples and popcorn. Music boomed over a loudspeaker, and there were tons of snack and game booths.

There were three other apple cider booths aside from Ashley's. They belonged to Felicia Jimenez, Owen McDonald, and Logan Beecham.

Ashley adjusted the sign hanging on her own cider booth. It was painted white and decorated with red paper apples and pink hearts and read:

Spice Up Your Life with Ashley's Apple Cider!

"Thanks for helping me, Elise," Ashley said as she poured cider into paper cups. "Just don't spill any glitter into the cider, okay?"

Elise was a total glitter freak. She wore glitter makeup and glitter clothes. She even used glittery toothpaste!

"I went easy on the glitter today," Elise said. She leaned on the counter of the booth and sighed. "Now if you only had some customers."

"Tell me about it." Ashley groaned. She pulled up the zipper on her hooded sweatshirt. "The festival started two hours ago and so far business stinks."

Ashley looked down the row of booths. About ten kids were already lined up for Logan Beecham's apple cider.

Logan wore a white chef's hat over his spiky blond hair and an apron over his tubby stomach. He grinned as he poured cup after cup of his golden brown cider.

Oh, great, Ashley thought. *The winning apple cider is chosen by how many kids line up for it. How can I win when everyone is lining up at Logan's booth?*

"What's Logan's secret?" Elise asked.

"Are you kidding?" Ashley asked. "Logan is the president of the Harrington Future Chefs of

America Club. He's a totally awesome cook."

Suddenly Logan stepped out from his booth. He cupped his hands around his mouth and shouted, "Might as well give up now, Burke!"

Elise put her hands on her hips. "If Logan Beecham can have a big mouth, so can we!" She leaned over the counter and shouted, "Check out Ashley's apple cider! It'll make your taste buds tingle with delight!"

Ashley giggled. "Try my apple cider!" she yelled. "It'll make your . . . tonsils tango!"

"All right!" Elise cheered.

Ashley saw Samantha Kramer and Philip Jacoby walking over. "Look who's coming," she whispered to Elise. "Samantha has had a major crush on Philip for months. But so far they're only friends."

"Bummer," Elise whispered back.

"Hi, guys," Ashley called to Samantha and Philip.

"Hi," Samantha said. "How about some of your tastebud-tingling cider?"

"Yeah," Philip said. "The line for Logan's cider is way long."

"Logan? Forget about Logan!" Elise cried. She held out two cups. "Ashley's cider is the best!"

Ashley watched as Samantha and Philip took the cups. They gulped down the cider.

11

"Well?" Ashley asked when they were finished. "What do you think?"

"It's really good," Philip said. He quickly turned to Samantha. "Hey, Sam. That new movie, *Big Apple Adventure*, is opening in town. Want to see it tonight?"

"Sure!" Samantha said. She gave Ashley and Elise a little wave as they walked off. "Thanks for the cider, guys!"

"Elise, I am in total shock," Ashley said. "Philip finally asked out Samantha."

"So?" Elise asked. "They *are* friends."

"News flash," Ashley declared. "Tonight is Saturday night. And Saturday night makes it an official date!"

Elise seemed to think about it. Then her eyes lit up. "Oh!" she said. "You're right!"

"Hey, Burke!" Logan called.

Ashley groaned. She turned to see him jumping up and down in front of the row of booths.

"I see you had two customers!" Logan shouted. "How much did you have to pay them to drink your cider? Ha, ha, haaaaa!"

Ashley was so angry, her cheeks burned. What was Logan's problem? Why couldn't he just leave them alone?

"Now I really want to win," Ashley said. "Just to show up Logan."

"And you *will* win," Elise said.

"With only two customers?" Ashley cried.

"Three," Elise said, pointing. "Here comes Cheryl. And she looks thirsty!"

Ashley turned. She saw her friend Cheryl Miller waving as she approached the booth.

"Hi, Cheryl," Ashley called.

"Want to try some of the world's best cider?" Elise asked.

"Bring it on!" Cheryl declared.

Ashley lifted the jug of cider and spotted Peter Juarez heading their way. Peter was a First Former at Harrington. He was also always teasing Cheryl.

"Better gulp it down fast, Cheryl," Ashley whispered. "Peter's coming."

"We know how much you hate him," Elise added. "He's always making fun of your red high-top sneakers."

Ashley glanced down at Cheryl's feet. Uh-oh. She was wearing those red sneakers again.

Cheryl took a small sip of the cider. She waited quietly until Peter approached the booth.

"What's up?" Peter asked. He and Cheryl exchanged a glance.

"Not much." Ashley poured him a cup of apple cider, and he took a gulp.

Cheryl took another sip of her cider. She and Peter were still eyeing each other while they drank.

Great, Ashley thought. *That's all I need—a fight right here at my booth. That should be perfect for business.*

"Hey, this is good stuff!" Peter declared.

He turned to Cheryl. But instead of insulting her, he put an arm around her shoulders!

"Want to go on the hayride?" Peter asked.

"Sure," Cheryl replied.

Ashley watched, stunned, as Cheryl and Peter walked away.

"Did you see that?" Elise cried. "Cheryl and Peter used to fight like cats and dogs. Now they're totally tight!"

"I saw it," Ashley said, shaking her head. "But I don't believe it."

Elise turned excitedly to Ashley. "Think about it, Ashley," she said. "First Samantha and Philip . . . now Cheryl and Peter. It's almost as if your apple cider is some kind of . . . love potion!"

A love potion, Ashley thought with a laugh. Now *that* would be good for business!

CHAPTER
THREE

I am so psyched! Mary-Kate thought as she dragged her duffel bag toward Ashley's room. *I can't believe Ashley and I are finally going to be roommates!*

It was Saturday night. Miss Viola had said it was okay for Mary-Kate and Ashley to share a room for a week. Phoebe had already moved her stuff into Mary-Kate and Campbell's room.

Now all I have to do is get Ashley to change her habits, Mary-Kate thought, *and I'll have clean laundry for a whole month!*

Mary-Kate knocked on the door.

"Who is it?" Ashley asked from inside the room.

"Your new roommate!" Mary-Kate answered.

The door flung wide open. Ashley yanked Mary-Kate into the room and gave her a big hug.

"Mary-Kate!" Ashley cried. She began jumping up and down. "This is going to be so cool!"

"Totally," Mary-Kate agreed. But the moment she looked over Ashley's shoulder her eyes widened. A gigantic stuffed giraffe was staring at her from across the room.

"Ashley?" Mary-Kate gulped. She pointed over Ashley's shoulder. "What is that?"

Ashley turned and smiled. "Mary-Kate," she said, "meet our third roomie—Mr. Stretch!"

"Mr. Stretch?" Mary-Kate repeated. She stared at the giraffe. His huge head almost reached the ceiling, thanks to his long, wobbly neck. His eyes and tongue bulged out, and he was also the color of old crusty mustard. Yuck!

"I picked him up at a garage sale last week," Ashley said proudly. "Isn't he way cool?"

Mary-Kate stared at the gigantic giraffe. He took up half the room. "Isn't he way . . . big?" she asked.

"Big and lovable!" Ashley said. She ran over to Mr. Stretch and hugged him around his long neck.

Uh-oh, Mary-Kate thought. *Why didn't Phoebe warn me about this?*

"Mary-Kate, I am so excited about us rooming together," Ashley said.

Okay, Mary-Kate thought. *If I'm going to start changing Ashley's habits and winning the bet, I'd better start right now.*

"Yeah," Mary-Kate said. "Now we can talk for hours and hours after lights-out."

"Oh, I don't think so," Ashley said. "Ever since we started White Oak, I've become a morning person."

"So . . . you don't stay up late anymore?" Mary-Kate asked slowly.

"Not really," Ashley said. She started to yawn. "Actually, I'm getting sleepy already."

Mary-Kate stared at her sister. Phoebe wasn't kidding about Ashley's going to bed early.

"I think working that cider booth wore me out," Ashley went on. "And get this—Elise called my cider a love potion."

"A love potion?" Mary-Kate laughed. "Why does she think that?"

"Two couples got together after drinking it," Ashley said. She headed for the door. "But if you ask me, it was just a fluke."

"Hey," Mary-Kate asked, "where are you going?"

"To wash up," Ashley said. She yawned again. "And then I'm hitting the sack. I even canceled my date with Ross because I'm so tired."

17

Mary-Kate glanced at the clock. It was only nine-thirty. And it was Saturday night!

This is more serious than I thought, Mary-Kate realized. How was she supposed to get Ashley to stay up past midnight?

Mary-Kate paced the room until her toe got stuck under one of Mr. Stretch's bulky feet. She gasped as she tripped and landed flat on her face.

"Ooooh!" Mary-Kate shouted. She shook a fist at Mr. Stretch. "I do *not* like you!"

She sat up and leaned against the bed. She tried to think of a way to make Ashley stay awake past midnight.

Ashley could stay up all night studying for a big killer test, Mary-Kate thought. *Nah. Ashley would probably want a good night's sleep instead.*

Or I could pretend to snore—super-loud, Mary-Kate decided. *Nah. I already snore. And that never kept her awake.*

Then suddenly it clicked. . . .

"Hey!" Mary-Kate said. "I'll have a party after lights-out. That should keep Ashley pumping past midnight!" She was interrupted by a knock on the door. "Who is it?" she called.

"It's your ex-roomie," Campbell said.

"And company," Phoebe added. "I can't believe I'm knocking on my own door."

"Come in," Mary-Kate called back.

"I see you've met Mr. Stretch," Phoebe said as she and Campbell entered the room. "Gross, isn't he?"

"How could I miss him?" Mary-Kate grumbled as she stood up. "So how do you two like being roommates?"

"It's cool," Campbell said.

Phoebe nodded. "I found out Campbell has a vintage football jersey from 1970." She modeled a blue and white shirt that had the number thirteen on the back.

"It was my dad's lucky jersey," Campbell explained. "So he never washed it."

Phoebe stared at her shirt in horror. "And you made me wear it?" she cried.

Campbell laughed. "I'm kidding!"

Mary-Kate laughed, too. She knew Campbell and Phoebe would hit it off.

"By the way, Mary-Kate," Campbell said. "We saw Ashley on her way to the showers. She looked tired."

"Really tired!" Phoebe teased. "In fact, I think I even saw her yawn."

"Big deal," Mary-Kate said, waving a hand. "I came up with a great way to prove that Ashley can stay up past midnight."

"You did?" Phoebe asked.

"Spill it," Campbell said.

Mary-Kate grinned from ear to ear. "Tomorrow night I'm going to throw a party," she explained. "A roomie reunion party."

"A party, huh?" Campbell said.

"And I'd like to throw it in your room," Mary-Kate said. "If it's okay with you guys."

"Okay with me," Phoebe said, shrugging.

"Me, too," Campbell said.

"Awesome!" Mary-Kate exclaimed. "We'll have chips, dip, music—"

"You're missing one thing," Campbell cut in.

"What?" Mary-Kate asked.

"Ashley!" Campbell said. "You'll never get her to come."

"Especially after a whole Sunday of pouring apple cider," Phoebe agreed.

But Mary-Kate wasn't worried. Since when did Ashley turn down an excuse for a good party?

"Ashley will be there," Mary-Kate insisted. "Just you wait!"

CHAPTER FOUR

"Thanks for helping me carry the cider, Mary-Kate," Ashley said on her way to her booth. She and Mary-Kate were each swinging two plastic jugs of cider as they made their way across campus.

The festival had started a few minutes earlier. Tons of kids were already filing through the yellow and red balloon arch toward the booths and games.

"By the way, Ashley," Mary-Kate said. "There's going to be a roomie reunion tonight in Campbell and Phoebe's room. There'll be chips and dip, music, some goofy games—"

"A party?" Ashley cried. "On a Sunday night?"

"A secret party," Mary-Kate whispered.

Ashley smiled. A roomie reunion *did* sound like a

neat idea. "Okay," she said. "I'll be there."

"Really?" Mary-Kate squeaked. "It's going to be after lights-out. It might even go past midnight. Are you sure you can stay up?"

Ashley shrugged. "Pretty sure."

"Cool!" Mary-Kate said.

Elise was already stacking paper cups when they reached Ashley's cider booth. Mary-Kate plunked her two jugs on the ledge and whispered to Ashley, "Sneak over to Campbell and Phoebe's room at ten-thirty tonight, okay?"

"I'm there," Ashley said.

"Great!" Mary-Kate cried. She waved as she ran off. "See you tonight, Ashley!"

Wow, Ashley thought. *Mary-Kate sure is psyched about this roomie reunion. I wonder if she misses Campbell.*

But Ashley didn't have time to think about the party. She had a cider booth to run!

"Hi, Elise," Ashley said, leaning over the counter. "Ready for business?"

Elise nodded. She pointed to a huge cup filled with cinnamon sticks. "And I set these up like you asked," she said. "Is cinnamon your secret ingredient, Ashley?"

"No." Ashley giggled. "But nice try! I just

thought it was a cool touch. Kids can put them in their cider if they want."

She was about to enter her booth when her boyfriend, Ross Lambert, came by. His brown hair hung over one eye, and he looked really cute in his faded jeans and denim jacket.

"Hi, Ross!" Ashley said. She was always happy to see him. "What's up?"

"Just wanted to wish you luck," Ross said, "and to try some of your prizewinning apple cider."

"I didn't win yet, Ross!" Ashley laughed. She gave him a cup and watched him gulp it down.

"So, Ross?" Elise asked. "What do you think of Ashley's apple cider?"

"It's sweet," Ross said. He leaned over and gave Ashley a kiss on the cheek. "Just like the cook. See you later, Ashley."

Ashley floated on a cloud as Ross waved and walked away.

"Yo, Burke!"

Ashley slowly turned around. Logan Beecham was standing just a few feet away. He was wearing a baker's hat and an apron that read: Beecham's Cider—good to the core!

"Now what, Logan?" Ashley asked.

Logan snapped his fingers. A boy dashed out

23

from inside his booth. It was Logan's roommate, Carl, holding a tray of brownies.

"Starting today, a free brownie will come with each cup of my apple cider," Logan announced.

"With nuts!" Carl added.

"I put two types of nuts into the batter," Logan said. "Pecans and walnuts . . . "

Ashley shook her head. "No fair, Logan!" she declared. "This is supposed to be a cider contest!"

Logan narrowed his eyes. "If you can have cinnamon sticks," he said, "I can have brownies."

"Don't worry, Ashley," Elise said as Logan and Carl marched back to their booth. "As soon as word gets out about your cider, we'll wipe the floor with Logan!"

"Yeah!" Ashley said. She took her place in the booth. She could see about six kids heading toward them already.

Maybe Elise is right, Ashley thought.

Soon more and more kids were flocking to her cider booth. Within two hours Ashley had about thirty thirsty customers.

"Coming right up!" Ashley called to the mob as she poured cup after cup of cider. Good thing Mary-Kate helped her lug all those jugs.

"What did I tell you?" Elise asked as she emptied the third jug. "Is this great or what?"

24

Ashley nodded. It sure was. But something wasn't adding up. . . .

"Elise?" Ashley said. "Have you noticed something weird about our customers?"

"Weird?" Elise asked. "What do you mean?"

"Most of them ask for two cups of apple cider," Ashley said, "instead of one."

"Hmm. It must be because it's so good," Elise said. "One cup of your awesome cider isn't enough, Ashley!"

"Thanks," Ashley said. "But I still don't get it."

"Hi, Ashley," Alyssa Fugi said as she hurried over. "I'll have two cups of cider, please."

Two again, Ashley thought as she filled the order. *People must really love my cider.*

"And I hope it works!" Alyssa added. She grabbed the two cups and hurried off.

"Hope it works?" Ashley repeated. "Elise, what do you think she meant by that?"

"I don't know," Elise said, shrugging.

Next Jeremy Burke strolled over. Jeremy was Ashley's cousin. He was also a bit of a pain.

"Hit me!" Jeremy said. He pointed to the jug of cider and grinned.

"Jeremy, this is your fifth cup of cider," Ashley said. "Are you that thirsty?"

"It's not for me," Jeremy said. "It's for the babes!" He took a cup from Elise and ran off.

Ashley blinked. "The babes? What is he talking about?"

"Um . . . er . . . " Elise said. "Some guys give girls flowers. Maybe Jeremy gives them apple cider."

Ashley stared at Elise. She was beginning to think something was going on.

"Ashley!" A voice interrupted her thoughts.

Ashley turned and saw their friend Summer Sorenson running over. She was tugging a cute-looking guy by the arm.

"Come on, Hunter," Summer was telling him. "You have to try some of Ashley's cider. It's the best!"

Hunter didn't answer. He was too busy bopping to the beat of his radio headset.

"I'll pour you a cup," Elise offered.

"Two, please!" Summer said, flipping her blond hair over her shoulder. She turned to Ashley and whispered, "Thanks, Ashley. I've wanted Hunter to like me for weeks!"

"Thanks for what?" Ashley asked, confused.

Summer leaned closer. "Thanks for your love potion," she whispered, her blue eyes sparkling.

"My what?" Ashley squeaked.

"As if you didn't know!" Summer laughed.

Summer and Hunter gulped down their cups of apple cider. Then they gazed into each other's eyes.

"Come on, Hunter," Summer said. "Let's carve some pumpkins into the shape of little hearts!"

"Cool," Hunter said, still bopping.

Ashley stared at Summer and Hunter as they walked off to the pumpkin-carving tent.

"If Summer thinks my cider is a love potion," Ashley thought out loud, "then maybe all those other kids think that my cider is a love potion, too."

Ashley quickly turned to Elise, who was looking everywhere except at Ashley.

"That's it!" Ashley cried. "Elise, did you tell everyone that my cider was a love potion?"

"No way!" Elise cried.

"Are you sure?" Ashley pressed her.

Elise dug her right foot into the dirt and dragged it around in a circle. "Weeeeell," she said slowly, "I told people that your cider *might* be a love potion. Huge difference."

Ashley groaned. No wonder tons of kids were storming her booth. They didn't want cider—they wanted love!

"How could you do that, Elise?" Ashley demanded.

"Well, who knows?" Elise asked. "Maybe your cider is a love potion, and—"

"It's not!" Ashley cut in.

"It could be," Elise insisted. "You gave some to Ross this morning. And right after he drank it, he kissed you."

"But Ross is my boyfriend," Ashley said. "That doesn't count!"

"Okay, okay." Elise sighed. "I know your cider isn't a love potion. I just thought a little rumor would be good for business, that's all."

"Oh, Elise!" Ashley groaned.

A group of Second Formers hurried over to the booth.

"Hi." Ashley forced a smile. "Would you like a cup of apple cider? That's cider—not love potion!"

"As if!" one girl said. "Jade Fellows gave a cup to Darren Nunzio, and he just asked her to go on the hayride."

"We don't know what you put in your cider, Ashley," another girl gushed, "but it sure seems to do the trick!"

"That's it!" Ashley said. "Elise, you watch the booth while I go set the record straight."

"You mean you're going to tell everyone your cider isn't a love potion?" Elise gasped.

Ashley nodded. But just as she was about to leave, she heard a familiar voice. . . .

"Ohhhhh, Burrrrrrke!"

Logan!

"My cider's going to beat your cider to a pulp!" Logan yelled. "A pulp. Get it?"

"He never lets up!" Ashley muttered.

"It's too bad, Ashley." Elise sighed. "A love potion would definitely help you beat Logan's cider."

Beat Logan? Ashley glanced toward the boy's booth. He and Carl had stuck cinnamon sticks up their noses and they were snorting like two walruses!

Ashley couldn't take it anymore. She had to put Logan in his place once and for all.

"Come to think of it," Ashley said slowly. "Maybe I'll just keep my big mouth shut!"

CHAPTER FIVE

"It's party time!" Mary-Kate cheered.

"Not so loud," Phoebe whispered. "If Miss Viola finds out we're having a party after lights-out, we'll be toast!"

Mary-Kate was pulling CDs from her rack. Campbell was blowing up balloons, and Phoebe was laying out plates of chips and dip. Everyone was wearing her coolest pajamas and slippers.

"Lights-out was ten minutes ago," Campbell said. "And I don't see Ashley anywhere."

"She's probably snug in her bed." Phoebe sighed. "Dreaming of blue ribbons and apple cider."

That better not be true, Mary-Kate thought. But she forced a smile. "That's what you think." She grabbed a chip. "Ashley will be here. Trust me."

Her eyes lit up when she heard someone knock on the door. "What did I tell you?" Mary-Kate said as she hurried to the door. But when she opened it, she gasped. Ashley was leaning against the door frame. She had dark circles under her eyes, and her hair was kind of messy.

"Five hundred cups of apple cider." Ashley groaned. "And this was just the second day."

Mary-Kate felt bad for Ashley. Her sister looked totally wiped out. But at the same time, she couldn't let her fall asleep!

Mary-Kate grabbed Ashley's arm and pulled her into the room. "It's time to party on!"

"You guys." Ashley yawned. "I'm totally beat. I just came here to say I'm not up for a party."

Phoebe and Campbell both smiled.

"Good idea," Campbell said. "After all that work, you really need your sleep."

"Yeah," Phoebe added. "Because tomorrow after classes you'll have to pour lots and lots of cider."

Mary-Kate began to panic. She had to do something—fast. "You can't go to sleep!" she cried.

"Why not?" Ashley yawned again.

"Um . . . because," Mary-Kate said. "We were just about to play charades."

"Charades?" Ashley repeated.

Mary-Kate nodded. Ashley couldn't fall asleep if she had to think!

"I'll go first," Campbell suggested.

"Now pay attention, Ashley," Mary-Kate said as she, Ashley, and Phoebe sat on the bed.

"Here goes," Campbell said. She pressed her palms together, then opened them up.

"It's a book!" Mary-Kate guessed.

Campbell nodded. She held up two fingers. Two words. Then she pressed her palms together again, this time against her cheek.

"Sleep?" Ashley asked wearily.

Campbell shook her head. She pointed at the night sky outside the window.

"Night? Good night?" Phoebe asked.

Uh-oh, Mary-Kate thought. Where was Campbell going with this?

Campbell pointed to the moon on her astrology poster.

"Is it . . . *Goodnight Moon*?" Ashley yawned.

"That's it!" Campbell snickered as Ashley lay back on the bed. *"Goodnight Moon!"*

Mary-Kate glared at Campbell. She'd picked a kids' bedtime book on purpose!

"You're next, Ashley," Mary-Kate said. She

grabbed Ashley's arm and pulled her off the bed.

"I don't want to play any more games," Ashley protested. "I told you. I'm tired."

"Fine," Mary-Kate said. She grabbed a bowl of dip and held it out. "Then try some of this jalapeño dip instead."

Ashley dug a nacho chip into the dip. But when she stuck it into her mouth—

"Whoa!" Ashley cried. She fanned her mouth. "This stuff is hot."

That should wake up Ashley, Mary-Kate thought. She glanced at the clock on the wall. Ten minutes to eleven. Twenty minutes down . . . one hour and ten minutes to go.

Ashley sat down on the rug with a cup of soda.

I know, Mary-Kate thought. *I'll pump Ashley with a ton of questions. That should keep her awake!*

"So, Ashley," Mary-Kate said. "How's the cider booth coming along? Do you think you'll win?"

"Well," Ashley said, "it's not so much about winning the prize anymore. It's more about beating Logan Beecham."

"You mean that obnoxious First Former from Harrington?" Phoebe asked.

"Yup," Ashley said. She yawned again.

Sleep alert! Mary-Kate thought. She dipped her

33

fingers into Ashley's soda. Then she splashed Ashley's face.

"Hey!" Ashley sputtered. "What's the big idea?"

"You were falling asleep," Mary-Kate said.

"Duh!" Ashley said. "I told you I was beat. And I have to get up at the crack of dawn to make more cider."

"Hey, Ashley," Mary-Kate said, "why don't I help you with the cider?"

"You?" Ashley smiled. "No offense, Mary-Kate, but you're not exactly Betty Crocker."

"Are you saying I can't cook?" Mary-Kate asked.

"Let's just say that the last time you made brownies," Ashley said, "they were more black than brown!"

"So they were a little burned." Mary-Kate shrugged. She gasped as Ashley headed for the door. "Where are you going?"

"To bed!" Ashley declared. "You guys will just have to party without me."

Campbell and Phoebe grinned at Mary-Kate.

"Remember, Mary-Kate," Campbell whispered. "My gym socks get washed in hot water."

"And my beaded cardigans need to be hand washed," Phoebe said.

"Ashley—wait!" Mary-Kate blurted out.

Ashley stopped at the door. "What now?"

"Um," Mary-Kate said. Her eyes darted around the room until they landed on her 4-You poster.

4-You was her favorite group—and Ashley's!

"There's a special live 4-You concert on the radio tonight," Mary-Kate said quickly. "It starts at twelve-thirty."

Mary-Kate held her breath as Ashley's tired eyes opened wide. Mary-Kate had made up the whole concert idea. But she was totally desperate!

"Did you say 4-You?" Ashley asked. "Live?"

"From Los Angeles," Mary-Kate added. "That's why it's on so late over here in New Hampshire. It's three hours earlier in California."

"Wow!" Ashley exclaimed. She walked back into the room. "This is something I have to stay up for!"

"Really?" Mary-Kate squeaked. She wanted to jump for joy. Her idea worked!

"You bet," Ashley said. She grabbed a disk and slipped it into the CD player. "So let's get this party started!"

Campbell and Phoebe stared at Mary-Kate. From the looks on their faces she could tell they didn't buy the concert idea.

Mary-Kate grinned and gave her friends a shrug. One challenge down . . . and only one to go!

CHAPTER SIX

"Hi," Ashley said as she trudged into her English class. She plopped down at the desk in front of her friend Wendy Linden. "What's up?"

Wendy stared at her. "I know you hate Mondays, Ashley, but you look awful!"

"Thanks." Ashley sighed. "I was up at five o'clock in the morning, making apple cider. And last night I was up past midnight, waiting for a 4-You concert on the radio."

"4-You?" Wendy asked excitedly. "Was it any good?"

"Who knows?" Ashley said. "It wasn't on. Mary-Kate said she must have gotten the concert date wrong."

Just then Lily Vanderhoff, another classmate, stopped at Ashley's desk.

"You're going to be at your cider booth this afternoon, right, Ashley?" Lily asked.

"Sure," Ashley said. "As soon as classes are over."

"Great!" Lily said. "Because I have a huge crush on this guy in my history class. He wants to save the whales, just like I do!"

Ashley rolled her eyes as Lily walked away. Did everyone at White Oak think her cider was a love potion?

"What was that all about?" Wendy asked. "I thought you were giving out apple cider."

"You mean you haven't heard?" Ashley said. "Half the kids in school think my apple cider is a love potion."

"How come?" Wendy asked.

"Oh, because some guys asked some girls out after drinking my cider," Ashley said. She shook her head. "As if my cider had anything to do with it!"

"I wish it did," Wendy muttered.

Ashley turned around in her seat. "Why, Wendy?" she asked. "Is there someone *you* like?"

Wendy glanced around, then leaned close to Ashley. "There's this guy in my math class," she whispered. "His name is Tyler Kelliher."

"I know Tyler," Ashley whispered back. "Doesn't he wear those crazy T-shirts? And he plays the clarinet in the Harrington School band, right?"

Wendy nodded. "I used to play the clarinet, too," she said. "I brought it up to White Oak, but I haven't opened the case in about two years."

"Cool," Ashley said. "So the two of you have something in common already."

"Big deal." Wendy sighed. "Tyler hardly knows I'm alive. I might as well be invisible."

Ashley smiled. Wendy could never be invisible. She was too much fun!

"Can you help me get Tyler's attention, Ashley?" Wendy asked.

"I'd love to help," Ashley said, "but I'm up to my neck in apple cider. I'm just too busy this week."

"I thought Elise was helping you," Wendy said.

"Elise works with me at the booth," Ashley explained. "But I could really use some help making the cider."

"Oh," Elise said. But then her eyes lit up. "I'll do it! I'm great in the kitchen. And I don't mind getting up early, either."

"Really?" Ashley asked. "That would be great."

"Come on, Ashley," Wendy said. "If you start

working on Tyler this afternoon, then I'll start working on your cider."

It was an offer Ashley couldn't refuse. "You got it," she agreed. "I'll show you my secret recipe during midday break."

"But don't let Tyler know I like him," Wendy said. "Not until we're sure he likes me."

"It's a deal!" Ashley said.

"Do you believe this incredible line?" Elise asked Ashley at the festival. "It snakes all the way back to the caramel popcorn stand!"

"I know!" Ashley said excitedly. "It's a good thing Wendy is helping us with the cider."

"You mean the love potion." Elise giggled.

"Very funny," Ashley said. While they finished setting up, she told Elise all about Wendy and Tyler.

"Yo, Burke!" a booming voice cut in.

Ashley turned to see Logan sitting inside his booth.

"I heard you put spider legs in your apple cider!" Logan shouted.

"You're so gross, Logan!" Ashley said. "You know that's not true. You're just jealous that I've got all these customers!"

"Shh!" Elise whispered. She nudged Ashley with

her elbow. "Here comes Mrs. Pritchard." Mrs. Pritchard was the headmistress at White Oak.

"Well!" Mrs. Pritchard said. She nodded at the long line. "You must have delicious apple cider, Ashley!"

"Would you like a cup, Mrs. Pritchard?" Ashley asked. She held up a jug. "It's the best!"

Mrs. Pritchard shook her head. "I'll leave the contest to the students," she said. "Keep up the good work."

"Even Mrs. Pritchard noticed," Ashley whispered excitedly to Elise. She turned back to her customers. "Next!"

"Hi," a boy said.

Ashley stared at the boy standing in front of her. He had curly black hair and was wearing a Mr. Bubble T-shirt.

"Tyler Kelliher!" Ashley gasped.

"That's me," Tyler said, smiling.

Am I lucky or what? Ashley thought. *I'll just pour Tyler some apple cider, then start talking about Wendy.*

"Have some cider, Tyler," Ashley said. She shoved a cup into his hand. "And stick around. I want to know what you think of it."

And what you think of Wendy! she silently added.

"Sure," Tyler said as he took a sip.

"So," Ashley said. "How is it?"

"This stuff is great," Tyler said.

"Have some more!" Ashley said, holding out another cup. "You know, you'll never guess who helped me with my cider, Tyler."

Tyler didn't respond.

"Um," Ashley went on. "Do you want to guess? She's a First Former like me. She's got really nice brown eyes and a great smile."

"I was wondering if maybe we could go on a date sometime, Ashley," Tyler blurted out.

Huh? Ashley jumped and splashed cider all over herself.

"Here you go," Tyler said, holding out a napkin.

But Ashley didn't care about the cider on her shirt. "What did you say?" she asked.

"I said maybe we could go out sometime," Tyler repeated.

Ashley sighed. "That's what I thought you said."

"Think about it," Tyler said. He crunched the cup in his hand and tossed it into the trash can. "See you!"

Ashley gaped at Tyler as he walked away. Something had gone terribly wrong.

"I heard that," Elise said over Ashley's shoulder. "He just asked you out!"

"But he's not supposed to ask me out." Ashley

groaned. "He's supposed to ask Wendy."

"Well, what do you expect?" Elise asked with a grin. "You're dealing with a highly effective love potion."

Ashley turned to face Elise. "Elise, quit saying that," she said. "My apple cider is not a love potion."

"Tell that to Tyler!" Elise laughed.

"Boy, do I have a problem," Ashley said. "How am I going to get Tyler to like Wendy when he seems to like me?"

CHAPTER SEVEN

"Are you sure it's that bad?" Mary-Kate asked.

"Worse than you can ever imagine," Phoebe replied. "I have to share a closet with Ashley, remember?"

Mary-Kate grabbed the handle on the closet door. She took a deep breath and turned to her friends. "Are you ready?" she asked. She hadn't dared to look inside Ashley's closet for months, but now she had no choice.

Phoebe and Campbell both nodded.

"Then stand back!" Mary-Kate shouted as she yanked the closet door open.

Everyone shrieked as shoes, sweaters, pants, and T-shirts tumbled out.

"It's an avalanche!" Campbell cried.

When the clothes settled on the floor, Mary-Kate stared at the towering heap. "Wow. I had no idea what I was dealing with," she said.

Mary-Kate plucked one of Ashley's hats from the floor and tossed it over Mr. Stretch's horns. "Here," she told the giraffe. "Make yourself useful for a change."

Phoebe folded her arms across her chest. "So, Mary-Kate," she said. "Do you know how you're going to get Ashley to clear out half her clothes?"

Mary-Kate nodded. "I've already come up with a plan."

"What is it?" Campbell said.

"Well," Mary-Kate said. "I know for a fact that the theater department needs new clothes for the costume room."

"So?" Campbell asked.

"So I'll ask Ashley to donate some of her clothes," Mary-Kate explained.

Campbell and Phoebe stared at Mary-Kate. Then they began to laugh.

"Ashley will never part with her wardrobe," Phoebe insisted.

"Wrong!" Mary-Kate declared. "I know for a fact that Ashley loves helping a good cause. She once

44

made fifteen cherry pies for a charity bake sale."

Mary-Kate, Campbell, and Phoebe began stuffing the clothes back into the closet. When they were done, Mary-Kate glared at Mr. Stretch.

"Do you see that?" Mary-Kate asked. "He stares at me while I do my homework, while I sleep. . . . What does he want from me now?"

"He's just a stuffed animal!" Campbell said.

"And you'd better deal with it, Mary-Kate," Phoebe said. "I don't like Mr. Stretch either, but Ashley loves him."

The door swung open. Ashley stepped into the room with a big yellow stain on her top.

"What happened to you?" Mary-Kate asked.

"Cider accident." Ashley sighed. She hurried toward the closet. "I just need a clean shirt."

Ashley opened the closet door a crack. She carefully slipped an arm inside and pulled out a salmon-colored long-sleeved T-shirt.

Wow, Mary-Kate thought. *She's got it down to a science!*

Ashley pointed to Mr. Stretch. "Hey! Why is my hat hanging on Mr. Stretch's horns?" she asked.

Mary-Kate froze. Ashley couldn't know they were studying her closet. "Um, no idea," she replied.

Ashley shrugged and stuffed the hat back into

45

her closet. "You know," she said, "after this Harvest Festival is over, I have to go shopping for winter clothes."

"Good idea," Campbell said. "As they say, one can never have too many clothes."

Mary-Kate glared at Campbell.

"Um, Ashley," Mary-Kate said. "Where are you going to put all those new clothes once you get them?"

"Where else?" Ashley asked. "In the closet."

"But you and Phoebe hardly have any room as it is," Mary-Kate pointed out. "So why don't you make room by getting rid of some of your clothes?"

While Ashley slipped into her clean shirt, Mary-Kate explained about the theater department and the donations.

"So what do you think?" Mary-Kate asked. She held her breath while Ashley thought it over.

"I think it's a neat idea," Ashley said. "Not only will I be clearing out my part of the closet, I'll be making a contribution to the White Oak theater department!"

"That's the idea!" Mary-Kate cheered.

"But I'll have to donate the clothes late this afternoon," Ashley said. "I still have a ton of cider to give out."

Ashley left the room.

Mary-Kate turned to Phoebe and Campbell and smiled. "I win! I win!"

"Not so fast," Phoebe said. "Ashley can still change her mind."

"In fact," Campbell added slowly, "if a bunch of Ashley's clothes aren't out of this closet by the end of the day, you lose."

"No problem," Mary-Kate said.

But by late afternoon, the closet was still jammed.

This doesn't look good, Mary-Kate thought. *I'd better go to Ashley's booth and see what's up.*

Mary-Kate ran across campus to the Harvest Festival. When she reached Ashley's booth, she had to squeeze through a thick crowd of kids to get to the front of the line.

"Sorry, Mary-Kate," Ashley said as she poured cup after cup of cider. "I'm too busy to sort through my clothes right now. I'll have to do it tomorrow."

Tomorrow? Mary-Kate's stomach flipped.

"I have an idea!" Mary-Kate blurted out. "Let me take your clothes over to the theater department."

"But I didn't pick them out yet," Ashley asked.

"Just tell me the ones you want to donate," Mary-Kate said, "and I'll get to work."

Ashley handed out four more cider cups.

"Okay," she said. "Take the old things from the back of the closet. Most of the stuff is on wire hangers."

"Back of closet . . . wire hangers," Mary-Kate repeated. "Got it."

Mary-Kate raced back to their room. She opened the closet door. Which side was Ashley's? Mary-Kate wasn't positive, but she had a feeling it was the right side. She reached way into the back. Sure enough, there was a bunch of things on wire hangers.

She yanked out an armload of clothes, pulled them off the wire hangers, and stuffed them into a big plastic garbage bag.

This was a piece of cake! Mary-Kate thought as she dragged the bag to the theater building.

"What's that?" Mrs. Tuttle asked as Mary-Kate dropped the bag on the costume room floor. Mrs. Tuttle was the head seamstress of the theater department.

"Here are some clothes for future performances," Mary-Kate announced. "I'd like to donate them to the theater department."

"Thank you, Mary-Kate," Mrs. Tuttle said. She pulled a pin out of a tomato-shaped pincushion. "We can always use more costumes for the plays."

Mary-Kate breathed a sigh of relief. Mission accomplished.

I did it! Mary-Kate thought as she walked back to Porter House. *I won the bet!*

As Mary-Kate neared her room, she spotted Phoebe waiting outside the door.

"There you are," Phoebe said. "I had to go inside my old room. But then I remembered that we switched keys."

Mary-Kate couldn't wait to tell Phoebe the news. "If you were planning to see if Ashley's clothes are still in the closet," she said, "you're out of luck."

"Why?" Phoebe asked.

Mary-Kate turned her key in the lock and opened the door. "Come in and see for yourself," she said.

"Okay," Phoebe said. "But I have to get my 1970s crocheted sweater from the closet."

Phoebe walked into the room and stuck her head into the closet. But instead of declaring how roomy it was, she began rummaging around.

"That's funny," Phoebe said. "I could have sworn my sweater was in here."

Mary-Kate stared at Phoebe. She was going through the right side of the closet—the side where Mary-Kate had taken the clothes!

"Um, Phoebe," Mary-Kate said, her voice cracking. "Do you by any chance use . . . wire hangers?"

"Sometimes," Phoebe said. "Why? Did you see my sweater?"

Mary-Kate's knees felt weak. She had donated Phoebe's clothes instead of Ashley's!

"Why don't I look for the sweater?" Mary-Kate squeaked.

"You?" Phoebe asked. "Why?"

"Because . . . er . . . I think I heard Miss Viola call your name out in the hall," Mary-Kate said quickly.

"Really?" Phoebe asked. "I must have a phone call."

"Right," Mary-Kate said. She hustled Phoebe into the hall. Then she slammed the door.

"Now I have to drag Ashley's clothes all the way to the theater building and switch them with Phoebe's!" Mary-Kate cried.

She looked at her watch and gasped. "And the building closes in five minutes!"

CHAPTER EIGHT

Mary-Kate pulled out another plastic garbage bag. She tore through the left side of the closet and stuffed the bag with some of Ashley's old clothes.

"Please let the building be open, please be open, please be open," she muttered as she dragged the bulky bag all the way across campus. But when she reached the door of the theater building . . .

"Oh, no!" Mary-Kate cried. "It's locked!" She dropped the bag. She leaned against the door and sank to the ground. "I lost the bet!" she wailed. "I'm going to be washing stinky socks for a whole month!"

The door suddenly swung open.

"Whoa!" Mary-Kate cried as she fell into the room.

Mrs. Tuttle peered down at Mary-Kate. "What can I do for you now?" she asked.

Mary-Kate sprung to her feet. She still had a chance to switch the bags!

"That bag of clothes I donated before was the wrong bag, Mrs. Tuttle," Mary-Kate said quickly. She pointed to the plastic bag outside the door. "That's the right bag."

Mrs. Tuttle looked at the bag. Then at Mary-Kate. "So what do you want me to do?" she asked.

"Um," Mary-Kate squeaked. "Can I . . . switch them?"

Mrs. Tuttle shrugged. "Go ahead," she said.

"Yes!" Mary-Kate cheered. "I mean, yes, Mrs. Tuttle, that's all I need to do."

Mrs. Tuttle held the door while Mary-Kate made the switch.

"I won!" Mary-Kate sighed as she dragged Phoebe's clothes back to Porter House. "But that was close!"

"How am I going to do it?" Ashley asked Mary-Kate that night. "How am I going to get Tyler to like Wendy instead of me?"

It was fifteen minutes after lights-out. Ashley and Mary-Kate were sitting up in bed and talking.

"Maybe Tyler and Wendy can go on a hayride,"

Mary-Kate said. "Hayrides can be pretty romantic."

Ashley gave it a thought. She and Ross once went on a hayride. And it was romantic. But . . .

"Wendy is allergic to hay." Ashley sighed.

"Oh," Mary-Kate said. "Then why doesn't Wendy buy Tyler one of those gooey caramel apples?"

"I don't think so," Ashley said. "Tyler wears braces."

Mary-Kate laughed. "Bad idea!"

Ashley giggled along with her sister. They were having fun together in the same room—just like old times. So much fun that Ashley wasn't even sleepy!

"Okay, back to square one," Mary-Kate said. "Is there anything that Tyler and Wendy have in common?"

"Yeah!" Ashley exclaimed. "Wendy and Tyler both play the clarinet."

"There you go!" Mary-Kate cheered. "Now all you have to do is figure out a way to let Tyler know."

Ashley was psyched. Why hadn't she thought of the clarinet before? She was about to plan a scheme when she heard music. A soft, jazzy kind of music.

Ashley swung her legs over the side of the bed as she listened. "That's really weird," she said.

"The music sounds like it's coming from outside."

"Who's playing music outside this late?" Mary-Kate asked. She jumped out of bed. But as she hurried to the window, she stumbled over one of Mr. Stretch's big stuffed feet!

"Ow!" Mary-Kate cried. "I hate that giraffe, Ashley!"

"Please. Nobody could hate Mr. Stretch!" Ashley replied. She walked to the window, lifted the blinds, and looked down.

"It's Tyler," Ashley said. He was wearing a tuxedo-print T-shirt under his black leather jacket. "And he's playing his clarinet."

Mary-Kate stared at him and giggled. "He looks like he's doing it for someone in our dorm," she said. "Just like in those old romantic movies."

Ashley gazed down at Tyler. Just then Tyler lowered his clarinet. He opened his mouth and began to sing.

"Ashley Burke . . . I must be a jerk . . . I never thought our love would work. . . ."

Ashley gasped. She knew Tyler had a little crush on her—but this was crazy!

"Uh-oh," Mary-Kate said. "How are you going to get Tyler to like Wendy now?"

"Wendy?" Ashley flopped down on her bed. She

threw her pillow over her head and moaned.

"Wendy lives right upstairs. She probably heard everything!"

Maybe Wendy slept through the whole thing, Ashley thought hopefully as she entered the Food Management Center.

"Good morning, Ashley," a voice said.

Ashley spun around. Standing behind her was Wendy.

"Hi, Wendy," Ashley said as they walked into the kitchen together. "Ready to make another batch of apple cider?"

"Sure," Wendy said. "As soon as you tell me why Tyler was singing a love song to you last night."

Ashley froze. *Uh-oh,* she thought.

Ashley smiled as she tied an apron over her red sweater and black jeans. "It was probably a rhyming assignment for his songwriting class. Burke . . . jerk . . . work. It's harder to rhyme Linden."

"Nice try, Ashley," Wendy said. "But I heard the whole thing from my window. You're supposed to get Tyler to notice me—not you!"

"Look, Wendy." Ashley sighed. "The whole thing was a misunderstanding."

Wendy frowned. "I thought you were supposed to be helping me, Ashley!"

"I am!" Ashley insisted. "And I came up with the perfect plan that's sure to get you and Tyler together."

"You did?" Wendy asked. She tilted her head. "What kind of a plan?"

Ashley grinned. "Meet me at the music building this afternoon at three o'clock sharp," she said. "And don't forget your clarinet!"

CHAPTER NINE

"Excuse me!" Mary-Kate said as she dragged her overstuffed laundry bag into Campbell and Phoebe's room. "Is this the drop-off laundry service?"

It was Tuesday during midday break. Phoebe was lying on her bed, reading a magazine. Campbell was typing on her computer.

"What is all that?" Campbell asked.

"What does it look like?" Mary-Kate replied. "It's this week's laundry. I won the bet, remember?"

"How can we forget?" Phoebe said. "You've been reminding us ever since you got Ashley to donate her clothes to the theater department."

"Didn't we hear enough bragging yesterday?" Campbell complained.

"Maybe," Mary-Kate said. "Now can I finally tell Ashley about the bet? She'll get such a kick out of it."

"To find out she was part of the bet?" Phoebe asked. She leaned back in her chair. "I don't think so!"

Mary-Kate pointed to her laundry bag. "Just remember," she said. "Make sure you wash all my red stuff separately."

"Okay, okay." Campbell groaned.

Mary-Kate smiled as she sat down on her old bed. The lumps were still in the same places. And the mattress still crunched. Just like old times!

"I can't believe it's already Tuesday." Mary-Kate sighed. "I'll be back here in my own room in no time."

"What about Ashley?" Phoebe asked. "Won't you miss rooming with her?"

"Sure," Mary-Kate said. "But there is one person I won't miss."

"Who?" Campbell asked.

"Mr. Stretch," Mary-Kate said.

"He's not a person!" Campbell laughed. "He's just a goofy stuffed giraffe."

"Don't tell that to Ashley," Mary-Kate said. "According to her, he rules the room."

"That's for sure," Phoebe replied. "Too bad we didn't make Mr. Stretch a part of the bet."

Suddenly a gleam appeared in Phoebe's eye. A smile began to spread across her face. "Why don't we reopen the bet?"

"No way," Mary-Kate declared. The mattress springs squeaked as she leaped off the bed. "The bet is over. And I won fair and square."

"I know, I know," Phoebe said. "But this time the prize will be double. If you win, then we do your laundry for *two* whole months."

Mary-Kate wasn't sure she liked the idea. What if she lost? Did that mean she had to do Campbell's and Phoebe's laundry for two months? But she wanted to hear Phoebe out.

"What do I have to do?" Mary-Kate asked.

"You have to get Ashley to give up Mr. Stretch," Phoebe said. "By Thursday after school."

"I don't know, Phoebe," Mary-Kate said.

"What's the matter?" Campbell said. "Don't think you can get rid of one little stuffed giraffe?"

"Whatever. It was just a suggestion," Phoebe said. Then she smiled. "But you know, Mary-Kate, Ashley loves that thing so much, she'll probably bring it home for winter break. And for the whole summer, too."

Mary-Kate's eyes flew wide open. Mr. Stretch? At home?

"Yeah," Campbell added. "Don't you guys share a room back in Chicago?"

"Okay, I'll do it!" Mary-Kate announced. It wouldn't be so hard. She had gotten Ashley to do everything so far, right?

Phoebe started to laugh.

"Hey," Mary-Kate said. "What's so funny?"

"No way will Ashley give up that giraffe," Phoebe said. "She adores him!"

"You'd better take your wash back, Mary-Kate," Campbell chuckled. "I don't think we'll be needing it anymore!"

Mary-Kate gulped as she watched her friends laughing. Of course Ashley adored Mr. Stretch. What was she thinking? How was she ever going to get Ashley to give up that giraffe?

CHAPTER TEN

"Now, remember, Wendy," Ashley said. "The plan is to show Tyler how much the two of you have in common. And that means playing the clarinet."

"But I haven't played this thing in years," Wendy said. She blew some dust off her clarinet case. "What if Tyler thinks I stink?"

"He won't," Ashley replied. "He'll be too busy wondering why he hasn't asked you out before."

Wendy raised an eyebrow. "Are you sure this is going to work?" she asked.

It better work, Ashley thought. But she flashed a confident smile. "Of course it will work!" she declared. "Trust me!"

Wendy sat on the steps of the music building.

Then she slowly opened her clarinet case.

Ashley checked her watch. It was three o'clock. "Tyler's music class ends right around now," she told Wendy. "So get ready to play."

"Thanks, Ashley," Wendy said. She smiled as she slid the reed into her clarinet. "But shouldn't you be working your cider booth?"

"Elise is watching the booth," Ashley explained. "And thanks to all the cider you helped me make, there's plenty to go around."

Wendy shut her case and held up her clarinet. "I think I'm ready," she said.

Ashley glanced over her shoulder at the music building. "I'll hide behind one of those pillars," she said. "But don't worry. I'll make sure Tyler never sees me."

Ashley slipped behind the closest pillar. She could hear Wendy begin to play a song.

Not bad, Ashley thought, peeking out. And as soon as Tyler came out, they'd be playing beautiful music together!

A few kids began to file out of the building. One of those kids was Tyler!

Ashley held her breath as he stopped behind Wendy. He shifted his clarinet case under his arm and grinned.

He's smiling! Ashley thought excitedly. *He's smiling at Wendy. The plan is working!* She strained her ears to listen.

"I didn't know you played the clarinet," Tyler said when Wendy stopped playing.

Wendy stood up and faced Tyler. "I haven't played in years," she admitted. "But I'd like to start practicing again."

"Cool," Tyler said. He gave a little shrug. "Maybe we could practice together sometime."

Ashley's heart did a triple flip. He'd practically asked Wendy out on a date!

Wendy smiled. "Well—"

"Say yes!" Ashley cried.

Tyler and Wendy spun around. Ashley clapped a hand over her mouth.

"Who's there?" Tyler called.

Ashley pounded the pillar with a fist. She had blown her cover!

"H-hi," Ashley stammered as she stepped into view. "Just . . . hanging out."

"Hi, Ashley," Wendy said.

"Wow!" Tyler gushed. "I never expected to see you around the music building, Ashley!"

"Oh, I just had to see where that awesome music was coming from," Ashley said. She turned to Tyler.

"Did you hear how well Wendy plays the clarinet?"

"Sure did," Tyler said.

"I can hardly believe that she hasn't practiced in years!" Ashley went on.

"Me either," Tyler said with a shrug.

"In fact," Ashley continued, "I wish I could play the clarinet just like Wendy. She's awesome!"

"Hey," Tyler said. "Maybe I could teach you how to play the clarinet, Ashley."

Ashley stared at Tyler. "What?"

"What?" Wendy cried.

Tyler nodded at Ashley. "We can meet during midday break," he said. "Or maybe even after school every day!"

Ashley began to panic. Her master plan was tanking!

"Thanks, Tyler," Ashley said quickly. "But with my cider booth and everything, I'm too busy during my breaks, and after school—"

"The Harvest Festival ends on Saturday," Tyler said. "So why don't we get together this Saturday night?"

"S-S-Saturday night?" Ashley stammered. "As in date night?"

"Yeah," Tyler said. "Unless you're already busy?"

"As a matter of fact, I am!" Ashley cried. "My boyfriend, Ross, mentioned going to the movies."

"Boyfriend?" Tyler asked. His smile turned into a frown. "Oh. Okay."

Ashley watched as Tyler trudged down the steps of the music building.

"Wait, Tyler!" Ashley called. "Aren't you and Wendy going to—"

Wendy jabbed Ashley with an elbow. "Forget it, Ashley. It's obvious who Tyler likes. And it's not me. Thanks for trying, though."

Ashley watched silently as Wendy packed up her clarinet. She felt awful. Wendy had gone out of her way to help her, but Ashley hadn't held up her end of the deal at all.

I've got to fix this, Ashley thought. *I've got to get Tyler and Wendy together if it's the last thing I do!*

CHAPTER ELEVEN

"So, Mary-Kate," Campbell said in the dining room Tuesday night. "Have you thought of a brilliant way to get Ashley to ditch Mr. Stretch?"

"Well," Mary-Kate said, "I'm going to tell Ashley about that plush-toy drive over at the children's hospital. I told you she loves to help good causes."

Campbell tore off a piece of her onion roll. "That is a good idea, Mary-Kate," she said.

"And it's a good cause," Mary-Kate added.

"There's just one problem," Phoebe said. "All of the plush animals have to be teddy bears for the hospital's annual teddy bear picnic."

"Teddy bears?" Mary-Kate groaned.

"Face it, Mary-Kate," Campbell said. "You're not

even anywhere close to getting rid of Mr. Stretch."

"Not true," Mary-Kate argued. "I have tons of great ideas. She tapped her head with one finger. "They're all in here."

Deep inside, Mary-Kate knew her friends were right. So far she had nothing. But she was not about to give up!

Mary-Kate finished her dinner and hurried back to her room. She had only one day to get Ashley to ditch Mr. Stretch!

If I stare at Mr. Stretch for hours, Mary-Kate thought as she opened the door, *something has got to click.*

Switching on the light, Mary-Kate gasped.

Ashley was sprawled on her bed with an open bag of chocolate chip cookies at her side.

Mary-Kate knew what that meant. Ashley always broke out the chocolate chip cookies when she was having a major crisis.

"Uh-oh," Mary-Kate said. "What's wrong?" She sat on the bed next to her. "Is it the cider?"

"That's the least of my problems." Ashley sighed. "It's Tyler Kelliher," she said. "The more I try to get him to like Wendy, the more he likes me!"

"Doesn't he know you already have a boyfriend?" Mary-Kate asked.

"He does now." Ashley sighed. "But what differ-ence does it make? Wendy has totally given up."

Mary-Kate watched as Ashley dug into the cookie bag. With Ashley so upset, how could Mary-Kate bring up Mr. Stretch?

"I'm sorry, Ashley," Mary-Kate said slowly. "If there's anything I can do for you—"

"There is!" Ashley interrupted. She sat up and pointed to Mary-Kate's side of the room. "You can start by cleaning up your mess."

"Mess?" Mary-Kate glanced at the books and clothes spread out on her bed. The sports equip-ment piled on her dresser. The balled-up tissues scattered on the floor. Her overflowing laundry bag. "What mess?"

"I love sharing a room with you, Mary-Kate," Ashley said. "But I forgot how messy your side can be. I mean, there's practically no room for any of my stuff!"

I'm *taking up too much room?* Mary-Kate immedi-ately thought of Mr. Stretch.

"You know, Ashley," Mary-Kate said. "Maybe it's not my stuff that's taking up all the room."

"What do you mean?" Ashley demanded.

"Maybe if the room was less cluttered," Mary-Kate said, "it wouldn't seem so messy."

Casually, Mary-Kate walked around the room. "For example," she said. "You can start by adding some more bookshelves above your desk."

Ashley nodded. "It's possible."

"And you can replace your bulky beanbag chair with a sleek, foldable butterfly chair," Mary-Kate went on.

"Good idea," Ashley replied.

"And . . . " Mary-Kate said slowly. "You might want to think about getting rid of the biggest thing in the room."

"What's that?" Ashley asked.

Mary-Kate shrugged. "Mr. Stretch?"

Ashley's eyes popped wide open. She ran to Mr. Stretch and wrapped her arms around his long, wobbly neck.

"No way!" Ashley said. "I would never give up Mr. Stretch!"

Mary-Kate gaped at Ashley as her sister hugged the goofy giraffe. There was no way she was going to win this bet. Why didn't she stop it while she still had the chance?

Now, for the next two months she'd be washing tons and tons of dirty, stinky laundry!

CHAPTER TWELVE

"Thanks for helping me carry the cider again, Mary-Kate," Ashley said as they both plunked crates of cider jugs inside Ashley's booth. It was Wednesday afternoon and the Harvest Festival was still going strong.

"No problem," Mary-Kate said. She pretended to flex her biceps. "I don't work out with the girls' softball team for nothing."

Ashley giggled. With all the trouble she was having with Tyler, it was great to see more of Mary-Kate!

"Well, good luck today," Mary-Kate said. She walked away.

Ashley turned and saw Elise pushing her way

through the festival crowd. Elise was carrying another big cup of cinnamon sticks.

"Way to go, Ashley," Elise said as she entered the booth. She pointed to the jugs of apple cider. "That's enough cider to feed an army. We won't run out today!"

"Yeah." Ashley sighed.

Elise tilted her head as she studied Ashley for a minute. "Ashley?" she asked slowly. "Why do you look so bummed out? Didn't Wendy help you this morning?"

"That's the problem," Ashley wailed. "She did help me make the cider. And so far I've done nothing to help her."

Elise shook her head. "Why don't you just tell Tyler that Wendy likes him—once and for all?"

"I can't," Ashley said. "I promised Wendy I wouldn't tell Tyler until we knew for sure he liked her."

"Okay," Elise said. "But this will cheer you up, Ashley. Check out the kids lining up at your booth!"

Ashley smiled when she saw the crowd. "Wow," she whispered. "I can't believe they still think my cider is a love potion."

"Who cares?" Elise whispered back. "Just keep thinking about that blue ribbon on Saturday. And about beating the pants off Logan Beecham."

Ashley nodded. But then she realized something. "Oh, Elise!" she said. "I forgot to bring extra packages of paper cups. I'll just run to the—"

"Yo, Burke!"

Ashley looked up and saw Logan shoving his way to the front of the line. What now?

"Hello, ladies!" Logan said. He leaned over the counter and grinned.

"What do you want, Beecham?" Elise demanded. "Can't you see we're busy?"

"Which is exactly why I came over," Logan said. "I want to see what all the fuss is about."

"What do you mean?" Ashley asked.

Logan held out one hand. "A cup of Ashley's apple cider, please!" he said.

Ashley narrowed her eyes at Logan. Why did he want to try her cider? So he could figure out her secret recipe?

"Don't do it, Ashley," Elise muttered. "He doesn't deserve your cider."

"If you don't give me a cup," Logan said in a singsong voice, "I'll tell Mrs. Pritchard!"

The last thing Ashley wanted was to get in trouble with Mrs. Pritchard.

"Okay, okay," Ashley said. She poured some

cider into a cup and handed it to Logan. "Knock yourself out."

Logan sniffed the cider. Then he took a sip and began swishing it inside his mouth.

"Well?" Elise asked. She placed her hands on her hips. Logan stopped swishing. Then—

"Pfleeeech!"

"Ewww!" The crowd jumped back as Logan spit a stream of apple cider to the ground.

Ashley stood frozen. She couldn't believe Logan could be so creepy!

"It needs something," Logan said as he walked away. "Maybe another pinch of spider legs."

Ashley was steaming mad. But no way would she let Logan Beecham get the better of her.

"Forget him, Elise," Ashley muttered. "I'm going to run to the Student U for more cups."

Ashley raced to the Student Union. She was about to head to the supply closet, when she spotted Tyler. He was listening to a portable CD player as he pasted flyers on the wall.

Maybe there's still a chance, Ashley thought. *Maybe I can still get Tyler to like Wendy. It's worth one last try.*

Ashley flashed a big smile as she walked over. "Hi, Tyler!" she called. "What are you listening to?"

Tyler pulled off his earphones. "It's 'Keep It

Real,' by the Wingnuts!" Tyler said. He pointed to his Wingnuts T-shirt. "I really like them. Do you?"

Ashley did. But the last thing she wanted was another reason for Tyler to like her.

"No way!" Ashley snapped. She marched over to the cabinet and began pulling out paper cups. "I hate the Wingnuts. In fact, I think they totally reek!"

Tyler began to laugh. "Don't worry, Ashley," he said. "I know you have a boyfriend."

Ashley blushed. Tyler had gotten the message yesterday. And he was being a good sport about it, too.

"What flyers are you hanging up, Tyler?" Ashley asked. "Something cool happening?"

"Yup!" Tyler said. He walked over and taped a flyer to the cabinet. "My music club is having a karaoke party. It's here in the Union tonight at eight."

"Karaoke?" Ashley asked. "Sounds like fun." *And like the perfect way to get Tyler and Wendy together,* she thought.

"Think you'll be there?" Tyler asked.

"I am so there!" Ashley said as she carried the paper cups to the door. "And I might even bring a friend!"

*   *   *

"Thanks for telling me about this, Ashley," Wendy said that night. "The last time I tried karaoke I had a blast."

Ashley and Wendy walked together to the Student Union. If Ashley had told Wendy about Tyler, she might not have come. So she decided to surprise her instead.

"Karaoke is cool," Ashley said. "Where else can you grab a mike and pretend you're a superstar?"

The Student U was already jumping with kids from White Oak and Harrington. Tyler was working the karaoke machine while a group of Second Form boys sang a number by 4-You.

"Oh, no, Ashley," Wendy whispered. "Tyler's here! What do I do?"

"Just be yourself," Ashley whispered back. She saw Tyler wave from across the room. He was wearing a T-shirt decorated with musical notes.

"Ashley, Wendy!" Tyler called. He held up the mike. "Want to give it a shot?"

"Not me, thanks," Ashley said.

"Wendy?" Tyler asked. "Are you as good at singing as you are with the clarinet?"

Wendy blushed. "Well, I—"

"Wen-dy! Wen-dy! Wen-dy!" the other kids began to chant.

"Go for it," Ashley told her.

Wendy smiled, stepped forward, and took the mike from Tyler.

"So what tune will it be?" Tyler asked.

"I don't know." Wendy shrugged. "How about . . . 'Keep it Real,' by the Wingnuts?"

"The Wingnuts!" Tyler said. He pressed a few buttons on the controls. "An excellent choice!"

For sure, Ashley thought. *Those two have more in common than I thought!*

Ashley watched the TV screen as a music video appeared. Soon the lyrics were displayed on the bottom of the screen. Wendy began to sing.

"'I never wanted you to love me. . . . All I really wanted was to keep it real. . . .'"

Ashley listened in amazement. Wendy had the most awesome voice. But then something even more amazing happened. Tyler grabbed another mike and sang along!

Tyler and Wendy smiled shyly at each other. When the song was over, the Student U went wild.

"Way to go!" Ashley cheered. Clapping, she ran over to Wendy and Tyler.

"I didn't know you liked the Wingnuts!" Tyler told Wendy.

"I didn't know you liked karaoke!" Wendy said.

Ashley grinned and stepped back. Way back. This time she was not going to get in the way.

Tyler handed the controls to another guy. Then he and Wendy walked off to the side.

Ashley sat with the others and watched some more karaoke. But the corner of her eye was glued on Tyler and Wendy. They talked a lot. And laughed a lot. And even sang another duet!

After the party, Tyler helped pack up the equipment. Wendy ran over to Ashley, her face glowing.

"So?" Ashley asked Wendy. "How long did it take before Tyler asked you out?"

"He didn't," Wendy said.

"Oh," Ashley said, disappointed.

"But we had the most awesome time!" Wendy said, her eyes shining. "And look what he gave me!"

"What?" Ashley asked.

Wendy held up a CD. "It's the Wingnuts' latest CD!" she said. "Tyler just picked it up in town, but he wanted me to have it. Do you believe it?"

"That's a good sign," Ashley pointed out.

"I wish I could give Tyler something," Wendy said. "But I don't have a clue what it should be."

"What kind of stuff does he like?" Ashley asked. "Movies? Books? Electronic games?"

"Giraffes," Wendy said.

"Giraffes?" Ashley wrinkled her nose.

Wendy nodded. "Ever since Tyler was a kid he loved giraffes," she said. "He had giraffe sheets, giraffe wallpaper, giraffe birthday cakes. He even confessed that he still collects stuffed giraffes. Isn't that cute?"

Ashley's eyes widened as she thought of Mr. Stretch. He was a giraffe. He was stuffed, too!

"So what do you think, Ashley?" Wendy asked. "Any ideas for the ideal gift?"

Ashley didn't know what to say. She knew Mr. Stretch would be the perfect gift for Wendy to give to Tyler.

But was she willing to give him up?

CHAPTER THIRTEEN

"Listen, giraffe!" Mary-Kate told Mr. Stretch. "In just a few minutes Campbell and Phoebe will come into this room. And if they see you and your big feet—I lose the bet!"

Mary-Kate grunted as she lifted Mr. Stretch. It was Thursday afternoon. And Ashley still hadn't ditched the giraffe.

Mary-Kate was totally desperate. There was only one thing left to do. "Come on." Mary-Kate grunted as she lifted Mr. Stretch. "You're going undercover!"

She tried shoving the giraffe under her bed, but his feet stuck out. She tried cramming Mr. Stretch into the closet, but his neck stuck out. She even tried putting a lamp shade over his head—but his tongue hung out!

"Why did you have to be so big?" Mary-Kate complained. "Why couldn't Ashley have picked up a stuffed squirrel?"

Mary-Kate glanced at her watch. If she worked fast enough, she still might be able to hide Mr. Stretch in another room.

"Come on," Mary-Kate said as she lifted the giraffe. She stumbled toward the door. But then she heard footsteps in the hall. And Campbell's and Phoebe's voices!

"Too late," Mary-Kate muttered.

There was a knock, and then the door swung open. Campbell and Phoebe walked into the room. Their eyes lit up when they saw Mr. Stretch.

"Campbell!" Phoebe cried. "Do you see what I see?"

"I sure do," Campbell said. "And you know what that means."

"It means," Phoebe said, "that we—"

"Hi, guys!" Ashley interrupted as she stepped into the room. She looked at Mr. Stretch. "What are you doing with my giraffe?"

"Nothing!" Mary-Kate blurted out. She squeezed Mr. Stretch around his neck. "I just needed a hug!"

"What are you doing here, Ashley?" Phoebe asked. "Aren't you usually at your cider booth around now?"

"Not today." Ashley threw back her shoulders. "I'm here on a mission. You were right about Mr. Stretch, Mary-Kate," she said. "He does take up a lot of room. And as much as I love him, I've decided that it's time to give him away."

Mary-Kate's eyes widened. This was totally unbelievable!

"I knew you'd come around, Ashley," Mary-Kate said, trying to sound as if she really believed it. "So, when are you giving him away?"

"Right now," Ashley said. "Unless you want to hold on to him a little longer."

Was she kidding? "No!" Mary-Kate cried. She tossed the big giraffe at Ashley. "I'm feeling much, much better now!"

Ashley gave Mary-Kate a puzzled look.

"You might want to rethink this, Ashley," Phoebe warned her.

"What if Mr. Stretch winds up in the wrong hands?" Campbell asked. "What if some kid sticks bubble gum all over him?"

"I don't think so." Ashley laughed. "Mr. Stretch is going to be in very good hands."

"Whose hands?" Phoebe asked.

"Who cares?" Mary-Kate said quickly. "As long as Mr. Stretch finds a good home!"

Mary-Kate whisked Ashley and Mr. Stretch out of the room. After closing the door, she turned to Campbell and Phoebe. Mary-Kate didn't know why Ashley had changed her mind, but at this point it didn't really matter.

"Well, you did it, Mary-Kate," Phoebe said. "You aced the ultimate test."

"You got Ashley to give away that goofy giraffe," Campbell said.

"Of course I did!" Mary-Kate grinned at her friends. "I said I would, didn't I?"

CHAPTER
FOURTEEN

"Nervous?" Mary-Kate asked.

"Are you kidding?" Ashley said. "If my mouth were any drier, it would be filled with sawdust!"

It was Friday afternoon. In just a few minutes the judging of the apple cider would begin.

This is it, Ashley thought. *This is the day I've been waiting for!*

Crowds of kids were gathering in front of a long table covered with a white tablecloth. On top of the table stood four cups of apple cider.

I wonder which one is mine, Ashley thought.

She spotted Elise in the crowd. Elise gave Ashley a thumbs-up. Then she saw Tyler and Wendy. They were laughing together and eating cotton candy.

Ashley smiled. Her latest strategy was a major success. Just minutes after Wendy gave Mr. Stretch to Tyler, he asked her out. For Saturday night!

Now all I have to do is win this contest, Ashley thought, *and everything will be perfect.*

"I'm sure you're going to win, Ashley," Mary-Kate whispered. "No other cider booth had such a huge turnout."

"I hope you're right," Ashley said. But deep inside she knew she had an excellent chance.

Logan, Ashley thought, *you are about to go down!*

But where was Logan? Ashley scanned the crowd. She saw the other contestants—Felicia and Owen—but not Logan.

"I wonder where Logan is," Ashley said.

"He probably can't stand the thought of losing," Mary-Kate joked. But then she pointed over Ashley's shoulder. "Wait. Isn't that Logan over there? With Mrs. Pritchard?"

"Where?" Ashley asked. She strained to see where Mary-Kate was pointing. Mrs. Pritchard was walking toward the judging table—with Logan Beecham right behind her.

Logan stared straight at Ashley. He had a sneaky look on his face.

What is he up to? Ashley wondered.

84

A student adjusted the microphone next to the judging table. Mrs. Pritchard stepped up to the mike and began to speak.

"Students," she said, "I have just been told that the popularity of one of the apple ciders might have been based on a rumor."

Ashley's blood turned to ice. Suddenly she knew what Logan was doing.

"Oh, no, Mary-Kate," Ashley whispered. "Logan is trying to get me disqualified."

"Rumors are unacceptable," Mrs. Pritchard said sternly. "So in order for this contest to be fair, we have planned a little taste test instead."

"A taste test?" Ashley gasped. She caught sight of Elise's face in the crowd. She looked as nervous as Ashley felt.

Everyone watched as a student placed a number in front of each of the four cups.

"Without knowing which apple cider is which," Mrs. Pritchard continued, "we will ask a group of First Formers to judge the best apple cider."

"Your apple cider is awesome," Mary-Kate said. "You still have a great chance!"

Ashley hoped Mary-Kate was right. She watched as five First Formers marched to the table, each carrying a small chalkboard.

As the judges sipped, Ashley wondered which cup was hers—and how much they liked it!

"Thank you, judges," Mrs. Pritchard said when they finished sampling the ciders. "You've tasted each cider recipe. Now please cast your votes."

While the judges scribbled on chalkboards, Ashley grabbed Mary-Kate's hand and gave it a squeeze. When the judges were done, they held up their boards one by one: #3 #2 #3 #3 #3.

Ashley quickly did the math. "Four votes for cup number three," she said. "But who is number three?"

Excited whispers filled the tent.

"And the winner of this year's apple cider contest is," Mrs. Pritchard announced, "Ashley Burke!"

"It's me! It's me!" Ashley gasped.

"You did it, Ashley!" Mary-Kate cried. "And Logan Beecham didn't even come close!"

"No fair!" Logan started to shout. "I want a recount! A recount!"

The crowd cheered as Mrs. Pritchard pinned a blue ribbon to Ashley's denim jacket. Then Ashley ran back to Mary-Kate and her friends.

"Way to go!" Mary-Kate cheered. She gave Ashley an enormous hug. "I told you your apple cider rules!"

Samantha Kramer tapped Ashley on the shoulder. "If everything was just a rumor," she said slowly, "does this mean your apple cider wasn't a love potion?"

"It wasn't." Ashley sighed. "Sorry, Samantha."

"I'm not!" Samantha said, flashing a huge smile. "That means Philip Jacoby really did like me. Cool!"

Next Jeremy sauntered over. "Hey, cuz," he said. "I knew your apple cider wasn't a love potion."

"You did?" Ashley asked.

"Of course," Jeremy said. "I was always a babe magnet!"

Ashley rolled her eyes. She and Mary-Kate walked together to the candy-apple stand.

"Tomorrow is Saturday, Ashley," Mary-Kate said. "Let's spend the whole day together and celebrate. We can see a movie in town, go for pizza and ice cream, shop till we drop—just the two of us."

Ashley thought it was a great idea, until she remembered something.

"What's to celebrate?" Ashley sighed. "You're moving out of my room this weekend. And then we'll hardly see each other again."

"True," Mary-Kate agreed. "But we shouldn't have to live together to see each other. From now on let's make more time just to hang out."

87

Ashley smiled. It was the best idea she had heard in days. "You got it!" She gave her sister a high five. "You and me. Just like old times!"

"Hey, Ashley?" Mary-Kate said. "I'll also let you in on a little secret tomorrow."

"A secret?" Ashley asked.

"Yeah." Mary-Kate sighed. "It's about this crazy bet I had going."

"Okay," Ashley said. "And I'll let you in on a little secret, too."

"What?" Mary-Kate asked.

"My secret recipe," Ashley replied. "For blue-ribbon apple cider!"

As they walked on, Ashley smiled down at her blue ribbon. Winning the apple cider contest was important.

But it was nowhere near as important as spending time with her sister!

RECIPE FOR SUCCESS

by Elise Van Hook

What's the recipe for success? Two barrels of apples, fifteen game booths, sixty students ready to have a good time, and a pinch of good weather! This year's Harvest Festival was the best White Oak and Harrington have ever seen. It was a blast and we wanted to take a moment to give you the highlights.

Let's see, which was the best one? Was it when Coach Salvatore accidentally fell into the dunking booth? Or when Brian Maloney got a walnut from Logan's free brownies stuck up his nose? I'm pretty sure most students would say it was when Mr. Frangianella mixed up the horses' lunch with his ice cream cone—and wound up eating some hay!

The biggest highlight of the week for me was when my friend Ashley Burke won the apple cider contest! Since I worked at Ashley's booth, I managed to score her cider recipe to print in the newspaper. (Don't worry, she said I could!) Here it is:

First she takes a gallon of apple cider and pours it into a saucepan. Then she sprinkles in a pinch of ginger, nutmeg, and three cloves. She heats on medium-high for about half an hour, stirring occasionally. Then she throws in six cinnamon sticks and cooks for another half hour. Once she's done, she has some kicked-up apple cider!

That's apple cider, folks. It's NOT a love potion!

GLAM GAB
Totally T-Shirts
by Ashley Burke

Fashion expert Ashley Burke

Tired of your plain old T-shirts? There are tons of ways you can dress up your tees to make them look funky and cool.

• **Go Graffiti!** That's write! Last Saturday we had a Go Graffiti party here at Porter House. It was super-fun—and super-simple! We all wore plain white tees. And we each brought along a permanent marker in our favorite color. Then we wrote all over our shirts! Here are some things I scribbled on Phoebe Cahill's shirt: BFF! 2 good 2 B 4-gotten! You can write or draw anything you want. And the best part is, penmanship doesn't matter!

• **Cut it up!** Get a little style into your wardrobe with the useful, yet often forgotten glamour tool, scissors! Cut a cute zigzag design to pump up the neckline of that boring tee. Or try cutting vertical strips at the bottom of your shirt. For a burst of color, slip a bead onto each strip and secure it with a knot at the end!

• **Snip and Sew!** Want to get that "gathered" look on your plain tees? Here's how to do it: take scissors and cut a row of tiny slits (no wider than a quarter) anywhere on your T-shirt. The two most common places for slits are up the middle of the front and up the sleeves, but you can put them anyplace you want. Then using a needle and some ribbon, weave the ribbon through the slits. Pull on the end of the ribbon, and the shirt will instantly look gathered. Just make sure to sew the ends of the ribbon to your shirt so it stays that way!

Take it from me—all three of these options will make your wardrobe tee-rific!

SLIP 'N' SLIDE
Ooze or Lose!
by Mary-Kate Burke

Sports pro Mary-Kate Burke

Okay, so we didn't get to

kick-off this year's Harvest Festival with a Harrington football game (thanks to a giant rainstorm). But I had a lot of fun at the "Oozefest" that happened instead!

For everybody who was at "the fest," we're having another one this Saturday. Yeah! For all those who have no idea what an Ooze-fest is, I'll give you a few hints of what it isn't: 1) It's not watching the Harrington guys slip down a muddy field for a touchdown. 2) It has nothing to do with the frog guts

we saw in Biology last week. And 3) It's not—repeat not—about that slime your kid brother always has dripping out his nose!

If you want to know what it is, I suggest you meet the other Oozers in front of the Harrington main building tomorrow at 3:00. See you there!

THE GET-REAL GIRL

Dear Get-Real Girl,

My roommate and I get along great. There's just one problem. She loves to

play the clarinet and practices all the time in our room! I don't mind it once in a while, but all the time is too much! I don't want to be mean, but how can I get her to stop the music?

Signed,
Tuned Out

Dear Tuned,

I hear you (and her—I live down the hall)! Why don't you offer to go over to the music hall with her and listen to her practice every once in a while? That way you'll be showing your support—and she'll get used to going over there to practice!

Signed,
Get-Real Girl

Dear Get-Real Girl,

Two weeks ago my boyfriend dumped me and I've been really sad ever since! I still play "our song" and keep his picture on my desk. I want to move on but I keep thinking that I'll never find anyone I like better. Help!

Signed,
Out of Love

Dear Out of Love,

Step #1: Get Real! There are tons of great guys out there to choose from—and plenty of time to meet them!

Step #2: Get Out There! There's no sense in sitting around moping all the time, especially when you could be out having fun with your friends. Besides, how will you be sure you'll never like anyone better until you meet some new people?

Signed,
Get-Real Girl

THE FIRST FORM BUZZ
by Dana Woletsky

Hanging around the Harvest Festival got me a lot more than some apples and a hayride. I managed to score some great gossip, too!

SS has got it bad for a First Former from Harrington. But I hear he's more interested in listening to his Walkman than listening to her!

Question: Aren't we a little old for stuffed animals? I guess AB isn't. Word around Porter House is that she's into stuffed animals in a BIG way!

Speaking of AB, a Harrington guy with the initials LB tells me that she spread rumors about her apple cider in order to win the contest. Come on, AB. Do you really expect us to believe you invented a love potion?

Then again, love *has* been in the air these days. A certain TK was seen serenading a lucky girl in Porter House the other night. WL wanted the song to be for her—but it was really for someone else!

Remember girls, if you want the scoop, you just gotta snoop!

UPCOMING CALENDAR
Fall/Winter

Clothing shortage alert! No, not in your closet—at the theater department! They really need some new clothes for their upcoming plays so be sure to get down there and donate some of yours today.

You say you want extra credit? Well, you'll have to do a bit more than clap some dusty erasers. And standing on one foot all term might get you in The Guinness Book of World Records, but it'll do nothing for your grades. So head on down to the program office and sign up for a three-week extra credit class. You'll be glad you did!

Ho! Ho! Holly Helpers is looking for members. Do some good for your fellow classmates and join! The sign-up sheet is posted on the bulletin board outside Mrs. Pritchard's office.

Want to be a pop star? Then stop singing into your hairbrush in front of the mirror. Try singing in

front of an audience instead! Karaoke. Student lounge. Friday night. Be there. Be discovered!

IT'S ALL IN THE STARS
Fall Horoscopes

Leo
(July 22-August 21)

You're always the one eager to make things happen—and you always have a plan to do it! But this month, don't get overexcited about your plans. Make sure to sit down and carefully think about what you're going to do so you don't make any mistakes. That way, when you put your plans into motion, you can sit back and enjoy the ride!

Virgo
(August 22-September 22)

Like the rest of us, deep down, Virgos have their insecurities. But this month, don't let your fears hold you back. Don't be afraid to be the center of attention, and don't be afraid you won't be able to accomplish your goal. If you put your mind to it, you can do anything!

Libra
(September 23-October 22)

Libras are some of the most ambitious people out there. You're smart and savvy and know how to get places! Just make sure that this month, you don't push yourself too hard. Save your energy for something else. Otherwise, you might burn out before you reach your goal!

PSST! Take a sneak peek
at

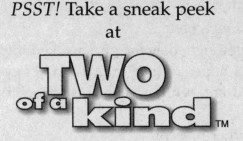

#26: The Perfect Gift

"Those earrings are awesome, Mary-Kate," Ashley Burke told her sister as they walked to biology class.

"I know!" Mary-Kate agreed. "My Secret Santa left them for me this morning."

"I got fresh-baked cookies from my Secret Santa," Ashley's roommate, Phoebe, put in. "They are sooo yummy."

"What did you get, Ashley?" Mary-Kate asked.

Ashley frowned. "A bologna sandwich," she replied.

"What?" Mary-Kate and Phoebe cried.

"I know," Ashley said. "It was really weird. I got this beautifully wrapped present. But I opened it up and found a half-eaten sandwich inside!"

Mary-Kate shrugged. "Maybe that was a joke gift," she suggested.

"Yeah," Phoebe agreed. "I bet your next present will be much better."

Ashley sighed as the girls walked into the classroom. "I hope so," she said. Then her eyes focused on a red-and-white striped package sitting on her desk.

Another present!

"There it is!" Ashley cried. She rushed to her desk and grabbed the package. Eagerly, she tore away the paper.

"Ewww!" she cried as she looked inside.

"What is it, Ashley?" Mary-Kate asked.

Ashley pinched her nose. "It's stinky gym socks!"

"Hmmm," Phoebe said. "Maybe I was wrong about this present being better."

What's going on here? Ashley wondered. *Why is someone leaving me nasty presents?*

There was only one answer. Someone didn't like her. But who was it?

Ashley was going to find out!

The Ultimate Fa

mary-kat

Don't miss

The New Adventures of MARY-KATE & ASHLEY™

Starring in

📖 HarperEntertainment
An Imprint of HarperCollins *Publishers*
www.harpercollins.com

PARACHUTE PRESS

DUALSTAR PUBLICATIONS

mary-kateandashley
America Online Keyword: mary-kate

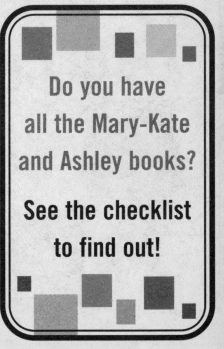

Do you have
all the Mary-Kate
and Ashley books?

**See the checklist
to find out!**

Mary-Kate and Ashley
Sweet 16
Licensed to Drive

#1 Girls Videogame Brand in America

It's How **YOU** Play.

- Exciting, multi-player, party-style fun
- Go cruising, earn your license and d the things you've only dreamed abou

mary-kateandashley.com
America Online Keyword: mary-kateandashley

With our Mary-Kate and Ashley **so little time** fashion dolls, you can have fun making our hit ABC Family series come to life.

Real Dolls for Real Girls

I play Chloe and I'm taking a painting class. You can help me finish this portrait with real paints.
–Ashley

I play Riley and I'm taking a photography class. You can help me develop fun photos.
–Mary-Kate

mary-kateandashley

mary-kateandashley.com
America Online Keyword: mary-kateandashley